Give Me Some

PHILIP BUNTING

Orchard Books
An Imprint of Scholastic Inc.
New York

Ever since the stars aligned to bring her here,
Una has loved space.

Her first step was
one giant leap.

Her first word
was "gravity"!

And with each birthday,
Una's cakes became
ascendingly astronomical.

Now, after a few more laps around the sun, Una lives in a world of cosmic curiosity and intergalactic inspiration.

The Moon.

Neil

Observation notebook

Actual meteorite!

Black hole.

Delicious!

Eat astronaut ice cream!

Orion.

Astronaut
Ice cream

Una dreams of a life in space.
Life on Earth is just so...so-so.

One day, Una will become an astronaut.
She will leave the Earth behind.

But for now, she is an Astronaut-in-Waiting.

Una very much likes the ASTRONAUT bit;
she is not so keen on the IN-WAITING part.
It will take eons to grow THIS TALL.

But here's the good bit. Una has been industriously working on an interplanetary plan...

Giant Party balloon

(H) or (He)?

Hydrogen?

Bun

Helmet must accommodate bun.

Don't forget to pack Astronaut ice cream.

Hmmm, I will need some boots.

Fig. 46:
Party balloon concept

Mars

Sun

Me

Moon

Earth

Jupiter

Fig. 23:
Escaping Earth's Pesky gravitational field

Astronaut ice cream

Fig. 3:
I bet Astronaut ice cream tastes even better in space.

with accompanying attire,
of course.

Fishbowl helmet
(sorry, Neil)

Hand-me-down
snowsuit from
big cousin Carl

Carl's **ski** gloves
(slightly too big
but they'll do
the trick)

Mum's dusty
all-white Uggs
(c. 1995).
Still cool

And today is the big day.

Today, Una will finally swap her humdrum, ho-hum life on Earth for an extraordinary, extraterrestrial life in space!

DIY oxygen tanks
(from recycling bin)

Juice. Juice.

Lots of tape
to hold things
together

Some pipes
from the shed

(Once she has packed a picnic and said so-long to Neil.)

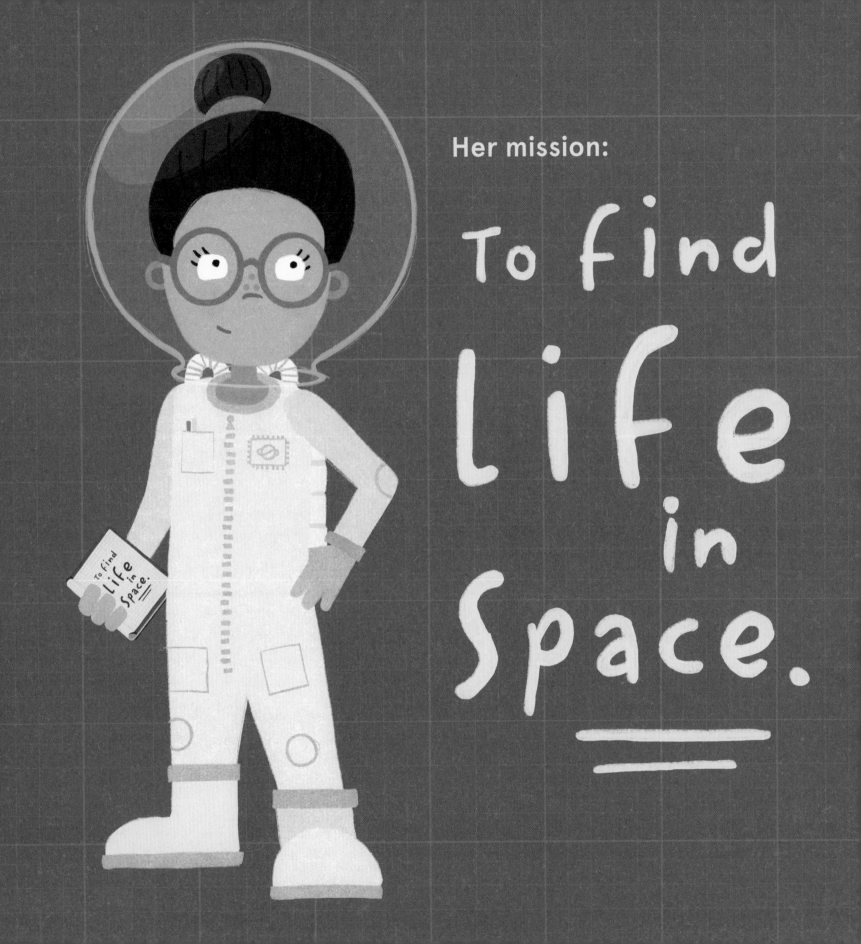

Her mission:

To find life in Space.

But she will have to get there first.

Attempt #1

~~Soda & mints~~

Fail!

Attempt #2

~~Giant party balloon filled with hydrogen~~

Nope.

Elevation: 32cm

Hydrogen.

Elevation: 56cm

→

(Ok, I might have jumped a little bit.)

Rocket!

Space was even more extraordinary than Una had hoped. There was no so-so. No humdrum. And certainly no ho-hum out here.

Mercury

A year on Mercury goes quickly! One Mercury year lasts just 88 Earth days. No life here though.

Venus

Venus is the hottest planet in the solar system with an average temperature of 465°C! That's way too toasty for life.

Saturn

No life here but one of its many moons (Titan) has its own atmosphere! Maybe one day...

Uranus

This smelly planet is shrouded by clouds of hydrogen sulphide (H_2S) — that's the stuff that makes rotten eggs stink. Pee-ew — too stinky for life to exist here.

← Titan

Jupiter

This whopper is 11 times wider than the Earth, and has at least 79 moons! But Jupiter is all gas, no life.

Mars

No life on the Red Planet (yet). But it is home to Olympus Mons — the tallest mountain in the Solar System — whose peak is over 26km above its base!

Almost at the edge
of the solar system.
No life so far ...

Phew, Uranus was
really SMELLY!

Am I alone
out here?

Did I remember
to feed Neil?

Maybe there is
no life
in space?

Una's mind expanded
like the universe with
each new moment.

Space and time seemed to stand still as she traveled farther toward the edge of the solar system.

Neptune

The most distant planet in our solar system is pretty **CHILLY** at an average of -214°C! No life here either. Brrrrr!

Kuiper Belt ↱

A giant donut-shaped ring of frozen rocks and ice. Pluto is in here, somewhere!

With all of this astronauting, Una had worked up quite an appetite. So she found a lovely spot on a ring of frozen rocks and launched into her cheese sandwiches and astronaut ice cream.

$C_3H_6O_2$

I've read that the center of the Milky Way tastes like **raspberries,** thanks to the compound ethyl formate. Yum!

In the distance, something caught Una's eye. Shining in the light of a nearby star, a tiny blue speck seemed to shimmer as if it were alive. Captivated, Una quickly packed up her picnic and set off toward it.

It spins
on its axis
at around
1,600km
per hour!

It's very **fast...**
Orbiting at 30km per second!

As she moved closer,
Una could see that
the shimmering blue
planet was orbiting
on a tremendous loop
around its star.

It has one
Moon.

It seems to be covered by
a very thin layer of **gas.**
An **atmosphere!**
Could this planet
support life?

What could it be? Had she discovered life in space?
A trillion possibilities rushed through Una's mind
as she approached the spinning, sparkling sphere.

And just like that, it came into sharp focus. The blue planet was ... the Earth.

Suspended in space, her beautiful blue home now shimmered even more brightly than before.

In that moment, Una made the most marvelous observation:

There is life in space...

We are life in space!

And we are all the crew of the most spectacular spaceship in the universe.

Everything we need
to **explore** the **COSMOS**
is already on board:

Fresh water

Air supply
(thanks, trees!)

Lots of
lovely food
(especially
astronaut
ice cream)

Plenty of room
to live, love,
learn, and play

Fellow
travelers
of all species,
shapes, and sizes

With her mission complete (and astronaut ice cream supplies severely depleted), it was time to return home... and begin a new mission.

We are all traveling
through **space** right now!
The Earth is our spaceship,
and it's the **only home** we've got.

It is **our mission** to
take care of the Earth
so that we can explore the universe
for **light-years to come.**

"I put up my thumb and shut one eye,
and my thumb blotted out the planet Earth.
I didn't feel like a giant. I felt very, very small."

Neil Armstrong ← Astronaut (not a goldfish)